Written and Illustrated by:

Mike Boldt

CreativeKiDs
publishing
ISBN 978-1-55454-455-4

Copyright © 2008 Creative Kids Publishing, a division of
Transglobal Communications Group, Inc.
5550 Skylane Boulevard, Suite G
Santa Rosa, CA 95403

Late one November night, Santa Bearclaws was busy checking over his list when there was a knock at his door.

Leonard, the head elf, came in with his usual ever-so-serious look. "Sir, there's a problem on the toy floor."

"The elves are not happy," Leonard explained. "They seem to think that the toy department is not as important as some of the others."

"Oh, what gave them that idea?" asked Santa.

"The reindeer," came Leonard's reply as he led Santa down the hall.

They arrived in the main toy making room just as the arguments were reaching their peak.

"Well, if it wasn't for the ELVES, there would be NO presents," came a shout.

"SO WHAT! If it wasn't for the REINDEER, the presents wouldn't be delivered!" was the stubborn reply.

"ALRIGHT! THAT'S ENOUGH!" Santa boomed over the shouting. "It's late and time for everyone to forget this nonsense and go home."

The mob of elves and reindeer settled down, mumbling and grumbling on their way out.

The next morning,
Santa Bearclaws arrived
at work early to find a
picket line in front of
his office.

"STRIKE! STRIKE!"
came the shouts of
the angry elves as
they hoisted signs
and marched around.

Leonard waded through the crowd to get to Santa. "This is a serious situation sir. If toy production is not restarted soon, we'll be behind schedule. Christmas is just one month away."

"You're right Leonard," Santa said. "It's time for a meeting."

That night, Leonard gathered everyone in the main hall. Before they could even start bickering, Santa spoke. "Here at the North Pole, I have a fantastic sleigh made of many parts. Now, if my sleigh didn't have a steering wheel or a rocket engine how well would it work?"

"It wouldn't work at all," came a reply from the back.

"That's exactly right!"
Santa said. "Yet the
rocket engine is no
more important than
the steering wheel or any
other part of the sleigh.
Our team works the same
way. Every department
is just as important as
the others in making
Christmas happen
every year!"

A murmur swept through the crowd on both sides and then one of the reindeer stepped forward. "Santa is right. If you elves didn't make all those toys, then we would have nothing to deliver. We depend on you."

"And we would have no way of delivering our toys without your work on the sleigh," replied the elves.

In the days following the meeting, there was a renewed effort by all and soon toy production was even ahead of schedule!

Santa Bearclaws was so happy that he threw a huge **Staff Appreciation** party to thank them. Everyone had a blast, even old Leonard.